THE ROAD TO
AFGHANISTAN

LINDA GRANFIELD

Illustrations by
BRIAN DEINES

North Winds Press

An Imprint of Scholastic Canada Ltd.

*With gratitude for the dedication of generations of Canadian service members and their families,
and with thanks to Sandy Bogart Johnston, who has generously travelled with me along the roads of history.* — LG

For Uncle Jeff, Uncle Mike and Jack. — BD

The paintings for this book were created in oil on linen.
The type was set in 18 point Filosofia.

Library and Archives Canada Cataloguing in Publication

Granfield, Linda
The road to Afghanistan / by Linda Granfield ; illustrated
by Brian Deines.

ISBN 978-1-4431-1356-4

1. Canada--History, Military--Juvenile fiction. 2. Soldiers--
Canada--Juvenile fiction. I. Deines, Brian II. Title.

PS8563.R356R62 2013   jC813'.54   C2012-907798-4

www.scholastic.ca

6 5 4 3 2 1   Printed in Malaysia 108   13 14 15 16 17

Afghanistan.

I've been there and seen the beauty of its mountains and its fields of wildflowers.

I've also seen the ugliness that war can bring to a country and to its people. I was a soldier there for two tours of duty, but now I'm home.

There have been other soldiers in my family.

When I was little, every November 11 my parents took my sister and me to the cemetery to place a wreath of red poppies on my great-grandfather's grave.

It was usually a cold, grey day.

When we got to the cemetery we stared at the name on the headstone: *John William Peterson.*

We said a prayer, left the wreath and drove back home, usually in the rain.

John William Peterson grew up in
Alberta, on the prairies, a farmer's son
who would one day inherit the family
land and grow wheat until he grew old.

But in 1914, as the sun brought harvest
time closer, a war began far away in
Europe. Young John went into town with
his friends and signed up to become a
soldier.

It was autumn. The young men said the
war would be over by Christmas. There
would be adventures to remember for the
rest of their lives.

They called it The Great War.

It wasn't so great after all. And it wasn't over by Christmas. John William spent nearly four years in the muddy fields of France. He fought in a town called Ypres — the soldiers called it "Wipers."

Bugs in his uniform made him itch. He ate canned meat and made tea in his metal hat.

He slept in a trench that filled with water and swimming rats when it rained.

He killed enemy soldiers and feared that he would be killed.

John William Peterson didn't die in The Great War.

But on one hot summer's day, on a battlefield that was once glorious with ripening wheat, an explosion changed his life.

He went home to Alberta without one of his arms.

Sometimes, in Afghanistan, I'd look out at the desert sands around me and think of my great-grandfather.

I'd watch the winds lifting the golden sand and grey dust and feel the heat rising from the earth, and I'd wonder about that farm boy standing knee-high in the crops that swayed in the prairie winds.

The boy who went to war as I did. The young man who returned and had to build a new life.

How could a man with one arm be a farmer?

There were ploughs to hook up to teams of horses, and machinery to operate.

Seeding and weeding. Scything and stooking.

Back-breaking work for a man with *two* hands. Too much for a man with one.

His younger brother took over the farm. And John William began a new life.

J.W. Peterson — Grocer said the sign on the store my great-grandfather owned.

Outside sat carts piled high with cabbages. The windows of the store were huge, with the prices of the goods shown on small squares of cardboard.

Cans were neatly stacked in a pyramid in the window. Imagine — a can of beans for just pennies, or a bag of flour for just over a quarter!

There's a lot you *can* do with one arm. You can place orders and stock shelves in a store. You can ring up the sales on the cash register.

You can find a new way to tie your shoes, button your shirt, cut your dinner on the plate . . . hold hands.

Emma Schultz packed the customers' purchases. Her parents had left Germany many years before to find a better life in Canada.

Emma became my great-grandmother.

John William found out that you don't need two arms to fall in love, to embrace your sweetheart . . . to hold your babies.

Sometimes, in Afghanistan, I was so afraid, I'd hear my heart thumping.

Sweat drenched my clothes. I heard screams.

I ran into clay buildings, alert for danger and hoping I'd get back out.

I couldn't sleep.

Even now, now that I'm home, some sounds make my heart thump.
Those sounds take me back to Afghanistan.
And I wonder if John William felt the same thumping and cold sweat
all those years ago.

We didn't go to Afghanistan just to fight.

We removed explosives and made roads safer for travel.

We helped build bridges and schools, dug wells, and brought security to places that for years had none.

And we shared games, candy and laughter with the children of Afghanistan.

Soldiers leave home and family to go to war. They come back changed.

The people who live where we fight, they suffer. They are changed, too. The French in 1914, during John William's war. The people of

Italy, where my grandfather, Arthur, fought in 1944 in the Second World War. And the Afghans, where I fought.

We all chose to become soldiers. We all had our reasons for making that choice. I wonder what theirs were. I know mine.

I didn't die in Afghanistan.

But on one hot, summer's day, on a quiet, dusty road, an explosion changed my life.

As I walked along, glancing towards the homes and watching for danger, I saw children peeking from the windows.

I smiled at one little boy and girl. I remember thinking how heavy my gear was, complaining to myself that we had too much to carry on such a stifling day.

I took my next step.

That step could have been my last.

Like one of my comrades, Brendan, I could have travelled home along the Highway of Heroes.

Many times people stood silently on the bridges over that highway. Some sang "O Canada" as the cars carrying the soldiers' coffins drove past.

In an Ottawa cemetery, marble gravestones mark where Brendan and other Canadian soldiers who died in Afghanistan are buried.
Above them, a Canadian flag snaps in blustery winds.
Like the winds I felt in Afghanistan.

On November 11 I visit the local memorial for remembrance ceremonies.

I wear a poppy and I think of the veterans in my family, like my dad's father, Arthur. And John William Peterson and the life he created for himself and his family.

I will need such courage for my journey to my new life.

Now I am a veteran with my own stories to share, when I am ready. Stories of a land far away and people I will never forget.

The children recite "In Flanders Fields" and lay a wreath of poppies at the memorial.

I am proud. And I cry a little.

Just a little.

On September 11, 2001, the World Trade Center in New York City was attacked and destroyed by al-Qaeda terrorists associated with the Taliban government of Afghanistan. Soon after, countries of the North Atlantic Treaty Organization (NATO) sent military forces to Afghanistan to bring stability to the country and to halt the training of terrorists. Canada sent its first combat troops in February 2002. The Canadians fought to reclaim areas from the Taliban, conducted patrols in search of improvised explosive devices (IEDs), and destroyed millions of land mines. During their tours of duty, service members also helped the Afghans access education and improve the irrigation of their fields.

The Canadian combat mission ended in July 2011. Canadians remained in Afghanistan as part of the NATO Training Mission, helping to train the Afghan National Army and Afghan National Police, who are responsible for Afghanistan's security when the NATO forces leave. This mission is scheduled for completion in 2014.

By the end of 2011, 158 Canadian soldiers had died in Afghanistan. One of them was Captain Nichola Goddard, the first female Canadian soldier killed in combat. More than 600 Canadians wounded in action returned home.

The physical injuries and post-traumatic stress disorder that many veterans suffer mirror what Canadian Forces personnel experienced in prior wars. While developments in medicine and technology are able to offer some help to our most recent veterans, they and their families will have much to remember, and perhaps much more to forget.

Sincere thanks to Brian Deines and to the following people who provided their expertise, support, and/or inspiration to this book: Diane Kerner, Aldo Fierro, and the whole Scholastic Canada team; Dominique Boulais, Commonwealth War Graves Commission; the Downey family; Major Sonny T. Hatton, 2nd Regiment, Royal Canadian Horse Artillery; Captain Jennifer C. Stadnyk, Public Affairs Officer, Canadian Expeditionary Force Command; Jean Marmoreo; Rosie DiManno; and finally, as ever, many thanks to Felicia Torchia, Cal, Devon and Brian Smiley for their loving support. — LG